-6 6-8

To David Alan Brubaker

Happy Sixth Birthday!

Much love,
   Aunt Grace

HIDDEN RICHES

ACORN SERIES No. 21

HIDDEN RICHES

by

MARIAN FELLOWS

VICTORY PRESS
LONDON AND EASTBOURNE

© Victory Press 1958

Reprinted 1966

Reprinted 1968

ISBN 0 85476 028 8

Printed in Great Britain for
VICTORY PRESS (Evangelical Publishers Ltd.),
Lottbridge Drove, Eastbourne, Sussex,
by Compton Printing Ltd.,
London and Aylesbury

CHAPTER ONE

Pauline awoke early, as the first bird was singing. She knew which bird it was—a kingfisher—a glorious creature with brilliant blue feathers and a yellow beak. Each morning he rent the quietness of dawn with his call. Afterwards came the grand chorus bursting in upon the new-born day from the throats of numberless smaller birds, brown, yellow and green. There were very large, ugly birds, too, with long, hooked beaks, which stole the babies of the yellow birds from their nests in the tall palm-trees. Sometimes she had seen the hawks, too, which swooped down on baby chicks and carried them off. These were not among this early morning symphony, so Pauline was able to lie in bed and enjoy it. Today was a special day, and she knew she must soon get up. She felt a heavy weight against her feet—a friendly kind of weight which was Tibby, asleep. She wiggled her toes against it, but it did not move. Through her mosquito net she could dimly see the small bed of her young brother Stephen, who still lay asleep. She was about to jump out of bed when her mother entered, quickly and quietly. That was the way Pauline always remembered her

5

mother—moving without much noise but getting many jobs done, and there were certainly many jobs, for Pauline's parents were missionaries.

"Good morning, dear," said Mrs. Rogers, drawing back the mosquito net and bracing herself for the violent hug which she knew would follow. She hugged her little girl in return, and as she did so she noticed a furry, black heap on the bed. "Oh, Pauline," she said reproachfully. "You've had Tibby on the bed again all night long."

Pauline continued to hug her mother, and with her face pressed against hers she said, "Yes, she crept in so quietly, and when I told her she mustn't sleep on my bed she didn't take any notice and she seemed a bit lonely so I let her stay."

"What nonsense," said Mrs. Rogers. "Now get up, because I want you out in record time so that the 'boys' can begin cleaning early. You know who is coming today."

So Pauline stood on the edge of the bed, held both her arms out sideways and leaped to the floor with a shriek of delight, her black, straight hair falling over her face and her eyes shining. She made such a noise she even woke Tibby, who yawned, arched her back, stretched and jumped softly to the floor. By this time Stephen, too, was awake and fumbling with his mosquito net. His large eyes peered through at Pauline.

"Why did you jump down like that?" he asked.

"Because I'm a bird," said Pauline, and she began singing gaily.

"What're you singing for?" asked Stephen petulantly, for he had not really woken up and felt cross because his mosquito net wouldn't respond to his attempts to remove it.

"I'm singing for the same reason," said Pauline.

"Tibby will eat you, then," said Stephen.

"No she won't, she loves me far too much," said Pauline.

Stephen banged his pillow. "Not as much as she loves me," he said hotly.

"Oh, yes, she loves me much more than that," laughed Pauline, knowing that Stephen looked upon Tibby as his own personal cat.

"I shall be a leopard, then," said Stephen, charging round inside his net until it suddenly gave way and he rolled off the bed.

Pauline laughed and laughed until she saw Stephen's face, then she tried to cheer him up. By now she was dressed, so she said, "Hurry up, Stephen, and I'll take you to see some new baby goats. They were only born yesterday, and it isn't very far."

Stephen cheered up promptly. He loved baby goats with their soft warm coats and long legs.

It was still very early when Pauline, looking like a new pin, stepped out on to the veranda.

She gazed thoughtfully at the glorious sky and wondered if it was too early to go over to Miss Brown's. She so wanted to tell her what was happening that day. Maybe if she walked over very slowly, by the time she reached there it would be almost time for the meeting with the schoolgirls, and Pauline would walk with her to the school.

So on this glorious morning Pauline slipped through the hibiscus hedge, whose bright red flowers were still wet with dew, and sauntered beneath tall palms and golden acacias gleaming in the bright African sun. Outside their neat mud houses Africans who lived on the compound were moving about, and some of the women were bathing squealing brown babies out of doors. They greeted Pauline as she passed, asking her in native fashion how she was, and Pauline replied politely, also native fashion, "Very well, thank you." Thus she reached Miss Brown's little house with its thatched roof and the rose-tree by the front door.

Miss Brown was sitting at a table when Pauline arrived, and she smiled, saying, "Why, how nice to see you, Pauline, so bright and early."

Pauline stood by her and leaned her arms on the table, looking up into Miss Brown's face.

"Do you know what's happening today?" she asked seriously.

8

Miss Brown said she thought lots of things might be happening, but didn't know which one Pauline meant.

"Do you know who is COMING today?" persevered Pauline, hoping that she didn't.

Miss Brown thought hard. "Who?" she asked at last.

Pauline's eyes were sparkling with the joy of bringing news, and she pushed back some stray black wisps of hair which had fallen over her face. Very confidentially she said, "The little girl from the Plantation."

Miss Brown's eyes opened wide, as though she were most surprised.

"Yes," Pauline went on. "Her daddy asked my daddy yesterday if she could come today, because he has to go away earlier than he expected. So daddy said of course it would be all right, because anyway we were expecting her soon. Her mother died you know."

"Yes," said Miss Brown seriously, for she knew all about the little girl at the Plantation who had lost her mother.

Pauline added, "Mummy says I'm to be a real sister to her and help her all I can, because she's probably very lonely."

"That is lovely," said Miss Brown, though in her heart she knew that the child from the Plantation, brought up amidst all the things that money

9

could buy, would be very different from the child standing by her now. "And what is her name?" she asked.

"Her name is Ann," replied Pauline, "and she will do school with me, and she can come to the meetings and get to know Rebeka."

"You must bring her along to tea one day," said Miss Brown.

"Oh, may I?" breathed Pauline, full of glorious dreams of the future. She would have someone of her own age with whom to play and work, someone who would be like a sister. It was lovely having Rebeka, and they played together often, but Rebeka was African, and they lived so differently. Ann would live in the same house.

The drum began to beat out its message, calling everyone to pray. Its deep voice boomed loud and rhythmically, and Pauline walked with Miss Brown to the neat little school, where the girls were to have their morning meeting. There was such a chattering inside until the message went round, "The white lady is coming", and then everyone stood to attention ready to greet Miss Brown. How nice they looked, all those happy brown faces, and how they sang, opening wide their mouths and showing white, flashing teeth. Pauline slipped in beside Rebeka and whispered, "I've something to tell you afterwards," which made Rebeka's big eyes open wider than ever. Miss

Brown taught Bible stories so nicely that even the most fidgety child would listen and enjoy them, but that day Rebeka could scarcely concentrate on Miss Brown or her story, wondering what Pauline's news could be. She sat swinging her slim brown legs and bare feet. She looked at Pauline's white socks and sandals and wished she could have some shoes—but even if she had them she would not wear them. Whatever would the others say? Some of the men wore shoes, but the women never did, not even on their wedding day. So Rebeka consoled herself with the thought that even if she had some beautiful shoes they would be no use to her. At last the meeting was over. They stood to sing a rousing hymn, Pauline said, "Good-bye," to Miss Brown, and then the two little girls walked off together hand in hand, for Rebeka did not live in the school like the boarders. Her father was the head-man on the compound, and so Rebeka lived at home.

Thus Pauline had the joy of telling the news to Rebeka, and she was amply rewarded when she saw the look of surprise on her face.

"Come round when they arrive," said Pauline grandly, "and I'll see that you shake hands with her."

The agreement was made, and Rebeka went home to tell her mother, and to ask that she might wear her best frock for the occasion.

Her mother said, "Well I never," and her eyes opened wide, just as Rebeka's had done, and she began calling out in the tribal language, so that before long everyone knew that another white child was coming to live there.

CHAPTER TWO

BY the time Pauline had finished confiding in Rebeka, which necessitated strolling leisurely along, and had afterwards stopped at several neat mud houses to inquire after a good many African babies, time had slipped by, so that on arriving home she found the family about to seat themselves at the breakfast-table, and a house-boy starting out to look for her.

"Run along quickly and wash your hands," said her mother, so away she went, stopping on the way to kiss her father because, she said, she hadn't seen him that morning.

She hurried back to the dining-room and took her place opposite Stephen, who stared across at her with enormous eyes and said, "You're late."

"Pooh!" said Pauline. "Can't you bear to wait a few seconds for your breakfast?"

But before the battle of words could continue Mr. Rogers held up his hand. "We will give thanks," he said quietly.

So they closed their eyes, except Stephen, who only screwed his up and squinted at Pauline. After the short prayer of thanks, Stephen could hardly wait a moment longer, so he said a very loud and definite "Amen" and attacked his fruit.

"Now go steady, old man," said his father.

"When the girl from the plantation comes," said Pauline, "Stephen will have to be more polite at table, won't he?"

"I shan't," said Stephen defiantly. "I don't care about the old girl from the plantation."

"But you will be nice to her," said his mother reprovingly. "She will live here like another sister."

"Don't want any more sisters," said Stephen. "And I'll not be nice to her."

"Of course you will," said his father. "Only ill-mannered boys talk like that."

"He's talking more like a little pagan than a Christian," said Pauline, enjoying seeing Stephen's wrath mounting.

"I don't care," grumbled the little boy, "and I don't want to be a Christian if I've got to keep on having sisters."

"Whatever is the matter with you this morning, Stephen?" cried his mother, helping him to a serving of porridge. "Now stop arguing and get on with your breakfast."

Stephen glared at Pauline, who, he could see, was silently laughing at him. "Horrid things," he said into his porridge, as though it was full of sisters.

To change the subject, Mr. Rogers said to Pauline, "You were off early this morning."

"Yes," she replied. "I wanted to tell Miss Brown about Ann. She says I'm to take her to tea one day." Her eyes sparkled, but she glanced in astonishment at Stephen, who said from the depths of his porridge plate:

"That's a good thing."

"What is?" everyone asked.

"I was thinking," said Stephen, once more the centre of the conversation, "that it will be a very good thing if she goes to tea with Miss Brown and dinner and breakfast too."

"How rude you are," cried Pauline. "I was only telling Miss Brown about you. . . ."

"Oh, you were, were you?" roared Stephen, before she could finish her sentence. "Well, you can just tell that old Miss Brown . . ."

But he never finished his sentence, for his father's strong hands lifted him bodily from his chair and deposited him outside.

"This is no place for you, young man," he said, and left him to the good-humoured teasing of the house-boys.

Back in the dining-room, Mrs. Rogers was wondering what had happened to disturb the family peace. Stephen and Pauline often quarrelled, but they usually knew why, and things could easily be straightened out. The scene at breakfast seemed quite unwarranted.

"Why ever is Stephen so difficult today of all

15

days?" she said. "Something must have upset him." She did not see the colour rise in Pauline's cheeks, but Mr. Rogers saw. He saw too that Pauline deliberately avoided her mother's eyes.

"Do you know, Pauline?" he asked quietly.

To Pauline, brought up to fear the telling of lies, it was extremely difficult to deceive her parents. She wanted to say No, she didn't know, but she could not, so she said in rather a small voice, "I think maybe I do." Only within the last few minutes had she remembered her promise to Stephen that morning. "I think he's annoyed because I promised to take him to see some baby goats, and I forgot him and went off early without him." She added, "He gets upset over such little things."

"But it isn't a little thing to Stephen," said her mother. "It would be nice afterwards if you went to apologise to him and say that you did not do it on purpose. He is probably very hurt."

"Apologise to him after all the things he's been saying," cried Pauline.

"Stephen is very young," continued her mother. "Anyway, you are the older one and should set a good example. Stephen takes notice of everything you do."

Pauline knew that her mother was right. She knew, too, that if she refused she would be miserable. Slowly she wandered out and found Stephen

16

quite happily feeding two cats with peanuts, Tibby and a large, thin, grey creature with ragged ears and a mournful expression. Without waiting for further discouragement, she began, "Stephen, I'm awfully sorry I didn't wait for you this morning. I quite forgot. But I'll take you to see the baby goats another time."

Stephen continued breaking peanuts. "I don't know that I shall want to go," he said loftily. Then he added, "Who told you to come and say that?"

Pauline tossed her head and walked away. She found her mother putting up fresh crisp curtains in Ann's room. A table stood near the window.

"Go and pick some flowers for Ann and put them in a vase," said Mrs. Rogers, so away ran Pauline, armed with scissors.

She went to the bed of zinnias, a mass of colour in the sunshine. Snip, snip went her scissors as she picked the best she could find, large, strong, glorious blooms of blues, mauves, pinks, yellows. "You are to cheer up a little girl who hasn't a mother," she whispered to them, as she arranged them in a vase and carried them to the bedroom. She enjoyed helping her mother. She heard the school bell and saw little brown feet flying to school. She would not be having school that day, which gave her a sense of freedom. It was exciting when a truck arrived during the morning with

Ann's bed, clothes and toys. Last of all, the men took off the truck a beautiful, shining bicycle—quite a small one, but, oh, so exciting. Stephen was fascinated, and followed the man to the box room where the toys were being put. He did not hear when his mother spoke to him. He was riding that beautiful, shining bicycle in his imagination, rushing madly around the compound to the cheers of the African children.

"You must not go into this room," said his mother, carefully closing the door, and leaving Stephen gazing at the forbidden room with greater curiosity than ever.

At last all was ready, and Pauline was dressed in her prettiest frock. After a long, long time came the car for which they had waited—a large, shining vehicle which drew almost silently up to the veranda of the house. Inside, almost out of sight, sat a small girl. Her father helped her out, and as she walked up to the veranda a murmur of admiration came from the natives who had gathered near by. Holding a large doll, she walked sedately up to the veranda steps. Pauline gazed enraptured at her golden curls, tied back with a broad blue ribbon, and her beautiful white, crisp frock decorated with ribbons and rose-buds.

Mr. Rogers was talking to Ann's father, and Mrs. Rogers welcomed the little girl, saying kindly, "We are so happy to have you with us, my dear."

18

As they all stood there, chatting, Mrs. Rogers suddenly noticed that Ann was standing next to Stephen. Remembering the conversation at breakfast, she went to lead the child away and over to Pauline, who stood shyly waiting for someone to introduce her.

However, before this could be accomplished, she saw Stephen already making himself known, and to her astonishment she heard him say in good imitation of herself, "Good afternoon, we are so happy to have you with us."

Pauline was so astonished she rushed up to her. "Did you hear what Stephen said?" she giggled.

"I certainly did," answered her mother, "and just look at his face, the rascal. Since he's seen Ann's bicycle he has become quite angelic. But go to her yourself, dear"; and Pauline, very shy and tongue-tied, went up to the other child.

"Hello," she said simply, and the two children stood staring at each other as though neither had a tongue in her head.

There was great excitement among the Africans as they sought to see the new white child. Along came the schoolgirls, marching smartly, ready to sing and welcome her. Drums could be heard approaching, and along came the schoolboys, equally ready to sing and welcome her. How well they sang. There was Rebeka, clean and smart in her best frock, singing merrily and moving her hands

to the rhythm of the tune. Pauline had almost forgotten Rebeka, but when the singing was over and
people were dispersing, and the grown-ups were
about to go into the house, suddenly a small, light
form skipped on to the veranda. It was Rebeka,
her large brown eyes shining. Pauline took
Rebeka's hand and led her over to Ann.

"This is Rebeka," she said, and Rebeka held
out a slim little hand, a little hand that, since
babyhood, had been used to greet friends both
black and white.

Poor Pauline was unprepared for the effect of
this hasty action. Ann stepped back and put her
hands behind her, as though scared that Rebeka
would touch her, and ran to her father. Trying to
hide the hurt, Rebeka turned and walked proudly
away, her black, curly head held high.

Pauline was so amazed that she did not think to
follow her, but let her go away. She had known
the Africans ever since she was born. Their
friendship and innate courtesy had surrounded
her every day. But that dainty Rebeka, with
whom she had so often played, should be so
insulted, was too much for her. Pauline's cheeks
burned with indignation. Her mother drew her
aside and asked her, "Why did you do that? It
would have been better to leave Ann to get used to
us first, before bringing Rebeka along. She isn't
used to the Africans as you are."

Pauline's dark eyes flashed, and she tossed back her hair with the impatient little gesture her mother knew so well. "I hate her," she said. "I hate her."

"Don't say that," said her mother, "or you are no better yourself. Of course you are sorry for Rebeka, but try to understand Ann too."

Mrs. Rogers sighed as she went back to her visitor. What a dreadful beginning. Poor Pauline was unhappy and disappointed, but she felt that if Ann was afraid of natives it was not her fault. How she must have been kept away from them, so different from her own children.

"If she so dislikes the Africans," thought Mrs. Rogers, "what memories of Africa will she have in future years? Would she ever be able to recall happiness she had known among the warm-hearted people of this great land?"

"What a big sigh," said Mr. Rogers later that night.

His wife smiled. "I was just wondering how Ann will fit in here," she said. "How different her life has been from that of our children. But of one thing we can be thankful, our two are already finding hidden riches of which Ann, as yet, knows nothing."

CHAPTER THREE

In spite of such a stormy beginning, Ann settled into life with the missionary family quietly enough. She had been very near to tears when her father left her, but was obviously determined to be brave about it. The next morning, after breakfast, she was astonished when Mr. Rogers fetched his large Bible and they all sat quietly listening as he read a passage of Scripture. She did not hear what he was reading, she was too busy watching the others, especially Stephen, who was examining her from over the other side of the table with his large eyes. She was more astonished when they all closed their eyes and Mr. Rogers prayed to God—just as though God were right there in the room. Stephen squinted at her through squeezed-up eyelids, and afterwards told his mother that Ann had never closed her eyes all through the prayer. "Which proves," said his mother, "that you didn't close your eyes, either."

Before breakfast Pauline, still smarting from Ann's behaviour the day before, had hurried over to Miss Brown's house, arriving with bright cheeks and black hair all awry. Sitting on a low stool with her chin in her hands, she came to the point of her visit without wasting time. "How can I be sorry for two people at the same time?" she inquired seriously.

"What do you mean?" asked Miss Brown.

"I mean, how can I feel sorry for Ann, when I am sorry for Rebeka because Ann was so rude to her yesterday? I was furious, but Mother says she is sorry for Ann," and Pauline's voice rose in indignation.

Miss Brown was silent for a few moments, then she said simply, "So am I."

Pauline sat bolt upright. "YOU?" she cried, her dark eyes wide with disappointment and amazement.

"Yes," went on her friend, "and I think you will feel sorry for her, too, if you only try to understand her."

"What do you mean?" asked the little girl.

Miss Brown's eyes were very kind and very wise as she tried to explain to Pauline. "We were very sorry that Rebeka was hurt, but we are sorry for Ann in quite a different way. You see, although Ann had a mother who allowed her to do almost everything she wished, and her father likes to give her everything money can buy—yet one thing she has not yet found."

"What is that?" asked Pauline.

"So far," explained Miss Brown, "she has not learnt to love people—and above all she has not learnt of the love of the Lord Jesus Christ. Both you and Rebeka have learned about Him all your lives, but Ann is quite in the dark—she needs you to help her to know Him."

These words of Miss Brown followed Pauline all the way home. "Ann is quite in the dark! She needs you . . ."

After breakfast Pauline went with Ann to the room where all her books and toys were stored. One by one boxes were opened, toys, dolls, books were brought out to be admired and duly returned except for Ann's present needs. Stephen, who had followed them, gazed enraptured at the large, bright picture-books as they appeared and disappeared, but above all he gazed at the bicycle standing there in all its glory. Maybe if he was very nice to her, Ann would let him ride it. Surely she had noticed how very polite he had been when she arrived—he had spoken to her just as his mother had done! It was with a thrill of joy, then, that he heard her say with a little toss of her fair curls, "You may come and see me ride my bicycle now."

Out they went, Pauline and Stephen dutifully watching as Ann showed how well she could ride. Round and round she went, the bicycle glinting and shining in the sun, Ann appearing more and more important each time she threw a glance at the two children. Pauline soon tired of watching, though she felt obliged to stay. It was then that she saw the goats—Mrs. Goat and her two black babies, trespassing on the mission compound, nibbling and chewing, the babies jumping and skipping, their tiny hooves tap-tapping ever so lightly.

"Oh, the darlings!" she exclaimed, and ignoring the suspicious glance of the mother, she picked up one tiny kid and pressed her cheek against the creature's soft, warm coat—so soft it was hard to believe it would one day be tough and shining like the mother's hard coat.

"Just you look here," called Pauline to Ann. "Don't you love them?"

"No, I don't," came the answer. "They're dirty, smelly things."

"They are NOT," cried Pauline indignantly, "not when they're so tiny. Just come and smell this one."

"That I won't," shouted Ann. "Oh, do look now, I'm riding without holding the handlebars. Do look."

Pauline ignored the invitation and gently put the tiny goat down, laughing as she watched it trying to find its land-legs again. "You would think I had bent its legs," she said, "they look so wobbly and crooked."

By this time Ann had dismounted. "It's terribly hot," she said, wheeling her bicycle into the shade.

Then seeing a house-boy appear for a moment she added, "Will you tell that boy to bring me my hat?"

Pauline left the goats to themselves. "Can't you fetch it yourself?" she asked crossly.

Ann's face flushed a little, but she only replied, "Mummy told me never to do anything if an African could do it for me."

Pauline forgot all she had heard at Miss Brown's. "Then you'll not like it here," she retorted. "Mother says we must never ask an African to do what we can do ourselves."

Suddenly Stephen rose to the occasion, to Pauline's surprise. "I'll fetch it," he said, and disappeared into the house.

Pauline wished she didn't feel so cross and disappointed with Ann. To try to appear friendly she started talking. "That's an awfully nice bicycle," she said, and putting out her hand, rang the bell. Its sharp, sweet sound resounded through the compound, but at the same time Ann reacted most strangely. Still feeling touchy after Pauline's rebuke, she drew away the bicycle and said, just as Stephen appeared with her hat, "Mummy said I was not to lend my bicycle to anyone."

Stephen stood still for a moment on hearing this, then, turning round, he went in again. Going to Ann's room, he threw her hat, her very beautiful and expensive hat, through the door towards her bed, and walked out. "You can fetch it yourself!" he mumbled ungraciously and went in search of other company.

Pauline decided to leave Ann to enjoy her bicycle on her own, and she went in search of Rebeka, whom she found carrying one large, plump baby on her hip, while a toddler clung to her hand. "You're not in school," stated Pauline.

"No," said Rebeka. "Mother wants me to mind the children while she's in the gardens."

Pauline took the hand of the toddler who had come up to her.

"I've just been watching Ann riding her bicycle," she said.

"Oh, have you?" said Rebeka. "Do you like having her live with you?"

"She says some queer things," said Pauline, "but I think it's because she has always been the only child. Mother says I must try to under-stand her." Then, having broached the subject of Ann, she said, "Mother says I ought not to have made you shake hands with Ann yesterday. All the same, I didn't like the way she refused you."

Rebeka shrugged her slim shoulders and hitched the fat baby farther on to her small hip so that she bent over the other way considerably, though she didn't seem to notice. "My mother says I ought not to have gone up to her the way I did," she explained candidly. "She says Ann isn't one of us."

"Ye-es," said Pauline thoughtfully, very pleased at having found this simple solution to the problem. She was so glad that no one seemed unduly worried over the affair. "I think you're quite right," she said, "and Miss Brown says we must help her because she doesn't know the Lord Jesus—probably doesn't even know much ABOUT Him."

"Is that so?" said Rebeka. "I thought all white children would know about Jesus."

Pauline returned to the house, wondering if her mother would be waiting to do school with her. Singing merrily, she entered the cool living-room, tossed her hat carelessly on to a chair and was about to call out to her mother when she heard her voice behind her.

"Come into my room at once, Pauline," said the voice, in a tone which made Pauline obey instantly.

Silently she followed her mother into the room, where Stephen was already waiting with a puzzled expression on his small round face. Mrs. Rogers sat down and did not speak for several seconds. She seemed to have some important news, but Pauline feared that it was not good news. At last she spoke.

"I am distressed to hear that my two children have treated our young visitor so badly on her first day," she explained.

Pauline and her brother exchanged inquiring glances.

Their mother went on, "Ann came to me in tears a short while ago. You, Pauline, have upset her very much with your words, and the fact that you went off and left her entirely to herself. As for you, Stephen, will you please tell me what right you have to ruin other people's property?"

Stephen's face was a picture. His eyes opened wide, his mouth did likewise, but he seemed incapable of speech. At last he was able to say, "I haven't ruined her hat."

His mother went then to the other side of the room and picked up an object. It was vaguely familiar to the children. It was a faint shadow of the expensive and beautiful hat belonging to Ann, but what had happened to it? Where were its beautiful flowers? The children gazed at it silently and solemnly.

At last Stephen said weakly, "I'm sure I never did that to it. I just threw it on to her bed."

"That," said his mother, "is where you are wrong. If you think you only threw it on to the bed you are mistaken. You threw it through the window. . . ."

". . . to the goats!" cried Pauline, finishing her mother's sentence.

"Yes," said Mrs. Rogers, "to the goats."

Stephen gasped, then both children began to giggle. They tried to be serious, but the more solemn their mother looked, the greater was the desire to giggle. Pauline even found herself wondering if the two kids had managed to eat any of the flowers. Their mother was not amused, and rebuked them sternly. They were to go and apologise. Pauline refused, saying it was Ann's own fault that she had been left. Stephen refused, saying he didn't do it on purpose. Pauline walked out of the room indignantly, and Stephen stumped after her. Their mother remained, sad that such a situation had arisen. How stubborn her two children could be. How difficult it would be if Ann wrote to her father in the way she had complained to Mrs. Rogers.

Pauline reached the room she and Stephen shared. She was hot and indignant, and for a while she stood silently gazing at nothing in particular, knowing that she ought to apologise, but furious that Ann had gone complaining to their mother. What would their father say? For a long time a battle raged in her young heart, but after a while she sighed and turned towards the door.

"It's no use, Stephen, we'll have to apologise,"

she said. "Miss Brown says we must help Ann, and I guess this is one of the ways of doing it."

Taking Stephen's unwilling hand, she dragged him after her. When the two children returned after a few minutes, Pauline felt light of heart, free and joyful as a bird.

"I feel better," she said. "Don't you feel better, Stephen?"

Stephen was busy emptying his small pockets of stones, pieces of string and ancient sweets.

"I don't think so," he said coolly.

"Oh, Stephen, I don't believe you have any feelings," cried his sister.

"I do, then," indignantly exclaimed the little boy. "I had feelings when mother said I'd given the goat Ann's old hat."

"Really," sighed Pauline. "I didn't mean THAT kind of feeling."

Back in Ann's room, no one knew of a little battle which was raging there too. No one knew with what relief the little girl had heard the other two children come to her door, nor the concealed delight with which she had heard Pauline apologise for them both. How lonely she felt, this little girl who had never had other children with whom to play. She did not know how to be friends, and had never learnt how to give as well as take. As the children went away she threw herself on her bed and sobbed bitterly, remembering her mother, wishing her father would come back, part of her wanting the children back again, part of her hating them for going away, and her cold, hungry little heart grew harder and more closed than ever.

CHAPTER FOUR

STEPHEN was having a wonderful time. Perched on the shoulders of a sturdy African, he was watching a football match, cheering and shouting with the others, though he never knew quite why they cheered when they did. However, an understanding of the rules of the game was quite unnecessary, for all rules seemed to have been abandoned long ago. One important fact remained —there was a football to be kicked, though there appeared to be no boundary and players continued kicking and pushing wherever the ball led them. Somehow, from time to time, the ball managed to be returned to the centre of the field. Occasionally there was a goal, followed by hilarious excitement, when players of both teams went wild, rushing around, throwing their arms about, some even rolling on the ground. Besides this was the general cheering and noise, some having found tin cans to bang. Stephen remembered that once he had watched his father teaching them the rules of the game. It was very orderly, but Stephen preferred tnis free interpretation, and was enjoying the general excitement and somehow managing to remain on the shoulders of this one spectator.

Suddenly he felt strong arms lift him down and found himself face to face with Musa, who insisted that he should return to the house. Stephen objected and Musa insisted. At last Musa won the day by placing the small boy on his own shoulders and jogging home with him, making funny little singing noises to the rhythm of his steps. Stephen enjoyed this, and arrived home flushed and excited.

It was during the meal that he heard the news of his father's safari. He was to be away two or three weeks. Stephen's spirits drooped. He did not want to be left behind.

"Dad," he said later, leaning against him and looking up into his face. "Dad, can I go with you?"

His father said certainly not.

Stephen sighed. "Must I stay here with all these girls?" he asked.

His father laughed and ruffled his hair. "I think you're a match for them any day," he said.

But Stephen was not so easily comforted. He knew that of late Ann had seemed to monopolise his mother. Often he had gone in search of her, only to find Ann already there, and being a very young boy he did not understand why he could not have his mother to himself sometimes. As for Ann, she resented the other children interrupting her little *tête-à-têtes* with Mrs. Rogers.

A few days after her father's departure, Pauline sat gazing at the distant patch of forest. "Let's go on a safari," she said suddenly.

"Where?" asked Stephen, who was standing with his hands thrust into his trouser pockets like a grown-up. He felt very important standing like this, especially as both Pauline and Ann were sitting on low stools. For once he could talk to them without having to look up at them.

Pauline waved a hand carelessly towards the forest. "Over there," she explained. "We can get to the forest in half an hour if we walk quickly, and if we don't go far in it will be all right."

"Who will take us?" asked Stephen, knowing the rules.

Pauline shrugged her shoulders. "Oh, Rebeka could take us. She knows the forest as well as anyone, and, after all, we're not going far."

Ann remained silent. "What d'you want to go there for?" she asked suspiciously.

"I don't know. Maybe it's because Daddy's gone somewhere in that direction," replied Pauline. "I don't see why we shouldn't be missionaries too. We might meet some pagans we can preach to."

This apparently did not appeal to Ann, but she saw Stephen eyeing her.

"Are you scared?" asked that small boy knowingly, and Ann tossed her head.

"Of course I'm not," she said.

Stephen persevered. "There's all kinds of things in the forest," he said.

"What kind of things?" asked Ann.

"Queer things."

Stephen watched Ann to see the reaction of this information upon her. Pauline could see that Stephen was discouraging Ann with purpose, but felt that they could not exclude her from their games and pleasures, especially after the incident of the hat.

"Don't be silly, Stephen," she said quickly. "You're just exaggerating."

"What's that?" asked Stephen innocently.

Pauline puckered her brow with the effort of explaining one word in terms of another.

"It means you're making it worse than it really is," she said, not realising that this statement of hers, far from encouraging Ann, only seemed to confirm the fact that there really were "queer things" in the forest. But the challenge had been thrown out, and she was not going to show fear in front of this little boy whom she could not bring herself to like, even if she tried. But as Ann never tried to like anyone, it was not likely that Stephen would find favour in her eyes easily.

Pauline really felt rather guilty as the little party reached the forest. She knew very well she was not obeying her mother at all, for her mother would never agree to Rebeka guiding them, however well Rebeka knew the twists and turns of the forest. But once inside the cool, green beauty of it, she forgot her fears and skipped along behind Rebeka, feeling as free as the birds which were singing lustily in the trees. How different everything seemed in the forest. Every sound was clearer. They stopped to listen to the strong notes of a bird calling far off, and somewhere they heard the crashing of branches way up above them as a monkey leapt from tree to tree. Overhead was green and yet more green, with sunlight filtering through gently. Oh, but it was good to be alive. They came to the mud which led down to the water. It was more than ordinary mud. The children knew that to fall in could be fatal if no one were around to help. Placed precariously over this boggy patch were numerous logs of varying sizes. Over these they went, Rebeka running lightly with sure feet, Pauline following holding Stephen's hand, though he objected to this humiliating assistance, being sure he could get across somewhere. How nimbly Rebeka had skipped across. He would like one day to be able to do the same. As they reached the other side of the mud and were ready to paddle through cool water they suddenly remembered Ann and, looking back, they saw her forlornly gazing at the treacherous logs before her. She had never crossed

such a bridge before. "All right, Ann," called
Pauline, "Rebeka will come and help you over.
Just hold on a minute."

But Ann felt too humiliated by such an offer,
and her proud young heart rebelled at being
different from the other children. So she started
across alone, balancing and wobbling.

"If you fall in," called out Stephen, "fall flat,
or else you'll go right in."

Pauline tittered at the idea of receiving such
encouragement in the middle of a bog. By this
time Rebeka had reached Ann, who, white and
shaky, received her helping hand gladly. Once
safely across, they all prepared to wade across the
water. Off came shoes and socks, Pauline and
Stephen rushing into the cool water with shouts of
delight. Ann regarded this process dubiously, but
could do no other than follow suit, though she
wondered what her mother would have said if she
had seen her taking off her shoes and socks in
company.

"Isn't it lovely?" called Pauline, and received
a good splashing from Stephen to prove that he
agreed.

Ann followed carefully but surely. On they
went, having put on shoes again and eventually
came to a felled tree.

"Let's sit here," said Pauline, so the children
sat in a row, listening to the forest noises. "There

don't seem to be any pagans to convert here," said Pauline, and turning to Rebeka, asked her if she knew of any pagans near by.

She spoke to Rebeka in the African language they all used, but Ann did not understand it, and each time felt left out, so that Pauline had to be careful to translate for her.

Rebeka said she thought there were some pigmies near by.

Pauline clapped her hands with joy. "Pigmies, how lovely," she cried. "Oh, do let's look for them."

Rebeka was a little doubtful. "They may have moved again," she said, "but if they are there you must let me go first, or they may run off when they see you."

On they went, and came to an opening through which Rebeka disappeared, holding up a restraining hand to the others. Stephen was very impressed with the secrecy of it, and felt obliged to talk in a whisper, which, however, was so loud that it would have attracted the attention of people quite a distance away.

"What'll you say to them?" he asked.

Pauline was thoughtful. She hadn't really considered this point.

"Well, I don't really know," she said frankly.

What would she say? It was one thing to pretend you were a missionary out to convert pagans, but another thing to decide what you should say. However, this problem was soon forgotten, for Rebeka returned with the news that there was a family living there and they had a child with a bad abscess on its leg. They went quietly towards the little clearing and saw the tiny, rather squalid dwellings of this little family. Pauline waited for Rebeka to welcome them on their behalf and then went forward rather shyly, but shyness disappeared as her eyes fell on the child with the ulcer. It was a horrible, tropical ulcer which had already eaten well into the little leg. She bent over it while the mother watched her suspiciously.

"Tell her," she said to Rebeka, "to bring the child to our dispensary for medicine, but ask her first if she will let me put a clean bandage on it to keep out the dirt."

Rebeka obliged, and the little woman murmured an acquiescence.

Dirt seemed to be everywhere. Pauline felt the responsibility of the situation, and called for boiled water. She watched while water was boiled in a rather doubtful-looking pot, then they waited for it to cool.

"What an awful place this is," said Ann, with a shudder.

"Is it?" said Pauline, who was thoroughly enjoying herself. "Now I think the water is cool enough. Come on, little one, and we'll clean this wound and dress it nicely."

Smiling at the mother, she took the little leg in one hand and poured the water over the wound. It was hot and the child cried, but Pauline was not the daughter of a nurse for nothing.

"Now it will be all right," she crooned, and something in her voice seemed to give the child confidence.

But how was she to bandage this ulcer? A quick thought sufficed. Off came a strip of her underskirt, while Ann and Rebeka gasped in astonishment. First she dabbed the wound with some of it, then she made a little pad with another portion, and with the rest she bound the leg neatly. By now all the other little pigmies had gathered round and were gazing at the spectacle of one of their number being treated by the white child. But when Pauline had finished and had turned to smile at them, it was as though she broke the spell, and they walked away, watching shyly from a safe distance.

"Now say to the mother that if she will bring her child to our dispensary we will soon heal this ulcer," said Pauline.

Rebeka translated this into the tribal dialect, and there was little more to be done.

Pauline, well pleased with the day's adventure,

suggested they start for home. "Won't Mother be glad we've been able to help the pigmies?" she said gaily.

Stephen grunted. "I don't think she'll be very pleased at your tearing your clothes up," he said dubiously.

As they walked back, Pauline suddenly realised what a long way they must have come. It seemed as if they would never reach the water. She realised, too, that it was getting dark, though she knew it soon became dark in the forest once the sun went down. She hoped it was not very late. What a lot of branches seemed to be getting under their feet, especially under Stephen's feet, for he found it difficult lifting his short legs high enough to avoid them. They were relieved when they saw the water. Off came shoes, and once over, they began to walk across the logs of wood. Rebeka led, holding Ann by the hand. Stephen followed, guided by Pauline. As they neared the end Stephen suddenly lost his balance. No one knew how it happened, but there was a shriek and Stephen was down in the horrible mud. Pauline screamed, and Rebeka in a twinkling had jumped on to the log nearest to him, but even so she could not reach his hand. Down she went on her front and managed to pull Stephen out a little. Pauline went to help and held on to Rebeka. It was a sad-looking Stephen who emerged, mud covered and miserable. Pauline rushed to hug him, but stopped at the sight of the mud.

"My you do smell queer," she said, "but, oh, Stephen, how worried I was when you fell in." She glanced at Rebeka and gasped. "Re-BEKA! Just look at your dress."

Rebeka did not need to look. She could feel the cold, sticky mud clinging to her through her thin dress.

Pauline was quite overcome with gratitude. "Rebeka, you saved my brother's life," she cried.

Rebeka was too busy with her frock to listen to any thanks. In a moment she had removed it and stood in her little skirt. They went farther to where they had passed a pool of water on their way in, and there they set about cleaning up Stephen, but the more they applied water, the muddier he seemed to become, and in the end Pauline was getting covered in mud herself. What a trio they were. Poor Stephen was nearly in tears. The shock of having fallen in the fatal mud and the subsequent humiliation was too much for him. Rebeka took his shoes and washed them, then washed his legs and feet. But his clothes remained a disgusting sight. At last they could wait no longer. They were sure it was getting steadily dimmer in the forest, and afraid of being caught there in the dark, they hurried on. All this time Ann felt like an outsider looking on at something which did not concern her. She listened as Pauline praised Rebeka and soothed Stephen, and wondered if it was not worth while falling in the mud to receive so much attention.

It was not so dark once they emerged from the forest, and soon they were near the compound. Already people were setting out to look for them, and as they approached there were gasps of amazement as the sorry-looking group drew near. Rebeka's mother was there, and immediately began scolding her child, partly through worry and anxiety, partly through fear of what Mrs. Rogers would say if this was Rebeka's fault. Very dejectedly the children walked home. Pauline and Stephen stood silently waiting for their mother's wrath to fall upon them. Her look of horror, on seeing Stephen covered in mud and Pauline not much better, was suddenly replaced by one of despair.

"What have you been up to?" she cried.

Pauline told her, not forgetting to add the story of the pigmies.

Mrs. Rogers ordered hot baths and then realised that Ann was standing there, neat and clean.

"Oh, what a blessing you are not in such a mess," she said, with great relief.

She hadn't the heart to punish them. They were already punished by their dreadful experience

44

in the mud. As she helped Pauline to remove her dirty clothes, she stared with curiosity at her underskirt. Pauline saw her expression and, going up to her, laid her cheek against that of her mother.

"Mummy, don't be cross. I tore that up to bandage the pigmy child."

Mrs. Rogers shook her head, and in spite of it all smiled to herself. After all, was that not the true missionary spirit? But she had to admit to herself that never had she sacrificed her own nice clothes for the sake of a native child, and remembering Ann's carefully preserved neatness in the midst of all these adventures, she wondered if, after all, it had been worth it. The muddy trio which returned with the scars of battle would be none the worse once they had slept off their tiredness, and would remember their adventure for many days to come.

She just said, "Remember, Pauline, that Stephen might have hurt himself badly. On no account must you disobey me again and go into the forest without my knowing."

Pauline nodded. "Yes, Mummy, I know it was very wrong of us. But you see, we wanted to pretend we were missionaries—and, after all, we did help the pigmies."

D

CHAPTER FIVE

ALTHOUGH the children had been disgracefully disobedient, the little trio of the mud adventure gained fame overnight. News always becomes distorted and exaggerated after it has passed from one person to another a few times, and Stephen found himself hero number one because he had apparently narrowly escaped death. Rebeka was second in importance because she had saved his life—this was published abroad by Pauline, who enjoyed telling people how wonderful Rebeka had been and how awful it had been to see Stephen "at death's door". So at school all the little girls wanted to walk with Rebeka and bathe in reflected glory, and Rebeka's level little head was almost turned through sudden all-round popularity.

At breakfast Ann retained an aloof silence. She was pathetically out of things, as some children seem always to be, though with a little less aloofness she would have often been more welcomed in the games of the others. Mrs. Rogers sighed and wished she could get a little closer to the girl's heart to understand her better, but in spite of the child's obvious preference for her company to that of the children, even she felt shut out. She watched Stephen now, as he sat regarding Ann with a cool, calculating stare.

Suddenly he said, as though Ann were not there, "Ann didn't get dirty yesterday, did she?" as if she had missed something rather special.

Ann's face flushed ever so slightly, and Mrs. Rogers tried to smooth things over with an appropriate light remark, but Stephen continued, in between large mouthfuls of toast and marmalade:

"Rebeka pulled me out, didn't she, Pauline? And Pauline held on to Rebeka, but Ann didn't do anything."

"Don't eat and talk at the same time," said Mrs. Rogers, "and I'm glad there is one child in this house who manages to keep clean. You and Pauline came home like little savages."

Stephen was not listening. He continued munching toast and regarding Ann, so that it was a good thing when the man appeared with the weekly post and letters were distributed. There was news from Daddy out in the bush, news from England, and Mrs. Rogers was glad to be able to pass a letter over to Ann from her father. It was all very exciting, and both Pauline and Stephen clamoured for news of their father, so that their mother had difficulty in reading the letter at all. Suddenly, in the midst of reading, she glanced at Ann, and was surprised at the expression on the little girl's face. It was not pleasant, and she wondered if her father had disappointed her in some way.

Breakfast over, Pauline called Stephen on to the veranda and sat him down on a chair while she stood before him. Stephen was suspicious—Pauline did not usually hold conferences on the veranda at that hour, and he waited patiently to hear what was on her mind. It was soon apparent that Pauline's missionary zeal had not abated, and in view of the lack of pagans near at hand, she had chosen Stephen as the object of her evangelical zeal. With her hands on her hips she stood over him menacingly.

"Now, Stephen," she began. "What did you think about when you tumbled in the bog yesterday?"

"I don't think I thought anything," said Stephen.

"Are you sure?" asked Pauline seriously. "Are you quite sure you didn't remember your past sins?"

"I don't think so," said Stephen. "Anyway, I haven't got any."

"Haven't got any," cried Pauline. "Oh, you poor boy. Who has been deceiving you?"

"Well, anyway, I didn't remember any yesterday," said Stephen.

"I read in a book," said Pauline thoughtfully,

"that when people are near to death all their past life comes before their eyes and they remember things they've done dozens of years ago."

She looked at Stephen solemnly, though he had so few years behind him, it would not take long to remember his whole lifetime.

"What would you have done if Rebeka and I hadn't been there?" asked Pauline.

"I wouldn't have been there either," retorted Stephen. "It was your idea."

"So it was," agreed Pauline, and Stephen thought he was to be released from this intense form of evangelism, but was disappointed when his sister began on a new line of approach.

"Stephen, you must be sure that you really are a Christian, and if you have any bad things in your heart you must let Jesus take them away."

Stephen gazed seriously into her face, but remained silent.

"Do you love everyone, for instance?" asked Pauline.

"Everyone?"

Pauline waved a hand to indicate the world in general. "Everyone," she repeated. "Jesus says we must love everyone, even our enemies. Now you love Mummy and Daddy. Do you love me?"

"I suppose so."

"And do you love Musa and Rebeka and all the other Africans here?"

Stephen nodded.

"And do you love Ann?"

Stephen stared hard into the distance. "Do I have to?" he asked.

"Yes."

"Well, I don't," he said defiantly. "She's an old meany, and look how she went telling tales the first day about her old hat."

Pauline shook her head. "You mustn't say things like that. We must try and love her—Miss Brown says so."

"Oh, Miss Brown," grumbled Stephen. "She doesn't have to live with her." Then he added, "There's something else I didn't tell you, 'cos I thought you wouldn't believe me."

"What is it?" asked Pauline, conscious that her little brother really had something on his mind.

Stephen's large eyes were very serious. "She tripped me up yesterday," he said quietly.

Pauline was too shocked for a moment to say anything, then she said a long drawn-out "O-oh!" She automatically dropped her voice as people do when speaking about unpleasant things. "You don't mean that, do you?"

Stephen nodded. "I do. She put her foot back and tripped me up. It was too dark to see properly, but I know she did."

Pauline forgot for a time all her promises to try to understand Ann. "If that is true," she said slowly and deliberately, "then she is a mean and horrible thing." Then she realised that if she went on like this she would begin to hate Ann, and she said, "But we've got to love her—somehow. I have asked Jesus to make me love her, and you must too, Stephen, because, after all, our parents are missionaries." She regarded him for a moment and then laughed softly. "She doesn't like you at all, does she, Stephen? You do annoy her you know. But let's go and forget about Ann for a bit. I'm going to write to Daddy, and you must write one too. I'll help you with it."

The two children went off, but they did not know that another little figure had hurried away just beforehand—a little figure that had been listening round the corner. Ann went to her room, hot and angry. Like all eavesdroppers, she had heard no good about herself and, having heard candid opinions, she was hurt and humiliated. Taking her father's letter, she re-read part of it, hot, angry tears welling up as she did so:

"I am enclosing two small cheques which I thought you could give to Pauline and Stephen at Easter—instead of Easter-eggs. They can choose what they like with the money. . . ."

Ann stamped her foot. "I'll not give them anything," she said, and pushed the two cheques
away. She gazed at them through her tears, and
suddenly snatching them up, she crumpled them
in her hands. "They'll never get them, never,"
she said, not realising that she was destroying
other people's property and was in reality stealing
their money. Little did she realise that although
no one else knew, she could not prevent her own
conscience from accusing her. Sitting down at the
table, she began a letter to her father:

"Dearest Daddy,
        "Thank you ever so much for your letter.
I do wish you would come back. The two
children here are not very nice and say things
about me behind my back and you know what
they did to my hat. . . ."

Meanwhile, Stephen was struggling with a
pencil, his brow puckered and his tongue working
from side to side as he did his best to write—but
it was so dreadful that we will not repeat his letter
here, for it was Stephen's very own spelling, which
no one else would understand.

Pauline chewed her pen a long while before
writing, then she composed a letter full of under-
linings and capital letters, so that her letter had the
appearance of being full of important phrases and

urgent messages. She told him about the pigmies and said, "I have decided that when I grow up *I'll* be a missionary among the *pigmies* so I hope I don't grow *TOO* big. I think they aren't so *afraid* of *small* people, don't you? I don't think Ann likes them. . . ."

CHAPTER SIX

THE children were having morning school under Mrs. Rogers' supervision, although Pauline was constantly gazing through the window watching and listening to the birds, and Stephen was secretly feeding Tibby with peanuts under his desk. They had that morning arranged a nice place for Tibby, because his mother said she would soon be having some kittens. So a good box was found, and an old piece of blanket, and the clean new bed put into a dark corner where Tibby could look after her babies unmolested. Since that hour, Stephen had gone five times to look at the box, hoping to see the kittens, and concerned that Tibby didn't lie there all day long, but wandered about quite unconcerned. She had followed him into school and rubbed against his legs until he had produced his usual supply of peanuts. His mother caught sight of these proceedings, and was just about to put Tibby out when a cry of surprise from Pauline made them all look in her direction. She was watching a small procession making its way to the house. Could it be—was it really—yes, surely it was. "It's the pigmies," she shouted joyfully. Sure enough, here

they were, led by Baba Eliya, who was all smiles.
How timid they looked, these little forest people.
There was the child with the bandaged leg, carried
by his mother. They all stood shyly gazing around
them, the children looking for all the world like
little goblins. Father carried his bow and arrows,
so did the little boys. "Oh, the darlings," said
Pauline, and rushed out with such speed that she
almost frightened them away.

Baba Eliya spoke for them. They had come
because the white child had invited them to receive
medicine for the ulcerated leg, but they would
return to their home immediately. Away everyone
went to the dispensary, even Ann, who did not
wish to be left out of the occasion. Carefully
Mrs. Rogers took away the bandage, now very
dirty, and revealed a horrible, raw, red wound,
from which pus was oozing. She cleaned the
wound and dressed it, and then gave an injection.
The child screamed with fright, and the parents
looked very concerned, but they did not say anything, and afterwards they went as quietly as they
had come, all the little goblins following with
serious little faces.

"Do you think they will come again?" asked
Pauline.

"I hope so," said her mother. "I told them they
must come for another injection, but we will see.
We never know with pigmies."

"I do think the pigmy children are sweet," said Pauline to Ann on the way back to the house.

"I don't," replied Ann. "I think they're dirty little things."

At lunch-time the post arrived, bringing a letter from Mr. Rogers. He was coming home the following Thursday. What excitement and joy for Pauline and Stephen, but poor Ann looked unhappy. How she wished it were her father who was coming.

"Daddy will be home for Easter," said Mrs. Rogers. "Isn't that lovely?"

Stephen sat gazing thoughtfully into space. "Do you think the kittens will come before Easter?" he asked.

"I don't know at all," said his mother, "and if you don't stop going to Tibby's box every few minutes she will get suspicious and not have her kittens here at all."

Everyone was glad to see the pigmies return for another injection. During their brief time on the station dear Baba Eliya took great pains to talk to them about the Lord Jesus, but their pagan minds were dark and closed, so that they did not really understand. They gazed at him with great eyes, and one day said yes, they believed that what he said was true, but Baba Eliya was sad because he knew they were only being polite.

It was the last time that the pigmies would come,

as the ulcer was quite healed now, the little leg hardly showed a mark where the great raw hole had been. They were all rather sad that it would be the last time, but to their surprise, when the family arrived, the father was carrying another, younger child, whom he handed to Mrs. Rogers. He was showing her that the child was sick and that she could heal him. Mrs. Rogers heard the difficult breathing of the little boy, and soon knew that he had pneumonia.

"It would be foolish to send the child away," she said. "Ask the parents if they will stay here so that we can care for him, and also save him from being carried about outside."

At first the parents refused, but when they heard that it might mean losing their child if they refused, they agreed, and a house was found for them, and a warm blanket for the sick child. Pauline insisted on visiting the patient, for, she said, the pigmies were probably less afraid of small people.

Stephen, too, out of curiosity, visited the little family and amazed his mother when he began to know some words of their language. It was at this time that Mrs. Rogers one day saw something queer hanging near the box which they had prepared for Tibby. It was a very dirty thing, and on coming closer she saw that it was an animal's tail.

57

"How disgusting," she cried, and quickly removed it and threw it well away from the house. She soon forgot it, for she was very busy. But when she found it again hanging there the next day she called Musa and inquired if he knew anything about it. He did not, neither did anyone else, so Musa was given instructions to burn the thing, but not near the house. However, Musa did not burn it immediately, and when he looked for it, it had disappeared.

That evening, on entering the children's room, Mrs. Rogers was horrified to see the thing under Stephen's bed, and Stephen was duly called.

"Stephen, what do you know about this thing?" she asked seriously.

Stephen looked at it with astonishment, as though he had never seen it before, but something prompted Mrs. Rogers to question him further.

"I got it from Tutu," he said.

"Whoever is Tutu?"

Stephen looked surprised. "The pigmy man of course," he said.

"But why ever did you want it?" asked his mother.

"It's to help Tibby have her kittens," explained the little boy.

Mrs. Rogers hardly knew what to say. Never had she imagined that by encouraging the little pigmy family to remain on the station, she was risking her little boy learning pagan customs.

"What did Tutu tell you about this?" she inquired. "And how did you get to know about it? We have never seen it in his house."

Stephen grinned. "He only puts it up when no one else is around. He knows when the nurse or Baba Eliya or you might visit him, and he takes it down. It was to help his little boy to get well."

Mrs. Rogers sighed. "Oh, Stephen," she said, 'don't you know these are the kind of things which we are fighting against? It is horrible pagan superstition, and Christians must never dabble in such things. We are asking the Lord Jesus to heal that little boy."

"He's a nice pigmy," said Stephen, by way of explanation.

"That may be so," replied his mother, "but that does not mean you should learn pagan customs from him. Now I forbid you to go to their house again."

Stephen looked up at her from beneath his dark lashes. "Do you want me to be like Ann?" he asked slyly. "The pigmies say everyone is nice and friendly to them but Ann."

"I shall speak to them myself," said his mother, and went straight away to call Baba Eliya and the African nurse. Together they explained to the mother and father that these pagan fetishes could not help their child, and that if they continued they might hinder the child's recovery.

Tutu stood politely to attention listening to this advice. "But our child isn't healed," he said.

"But he will be," explained Mrs. Rogers, "if you will only leave him to us. We are asking the Lord Jesus to heal him, and he is getting the best medicine possible. Please do not destroy all our work by bringing pagan customs on to the station."

Things went smoothly for a day or two, and although progress was slow, the child was certainly getting better. Then all at once it seemed as if the child slipped right back and became more ill than ever. Mrs. Rogers could not understand it, but Baba Eliya came to see her.

"White lady," he said seriously, "that child has had native medicine."

"But how?" asked the white lady.

It had been given by a pigmy who had visited the family and stayed one night. As a result the child lay very sick and with a high temperature.

"What can we do?" cried Mrs. Rogers, almost in tears. "We must pray and do all we can in our power to help him. Even yet these people shall learn that our God is more powerful than their pagan medicine."

She visited them again. "Your child is very,

very ill as a result of native medicine," she explained. "If you persist in this, he will die. We will try again to save him, but if you hinder our work in this way we cannot say what will happen."

The pigmies looked very serious about it and promised to obey. Now that they saw what native medicine had done for their child, they were prepared to leave it to the missionary.

Mr. Rogers returned on the Thursday. The children were so excited. They had so much to tell him. Ann was very quiet, and in spite of the efforts of the missionaries to draw her out of herself, she remained rather aloof.

"I'm tired of it all," she said to herself. "All this talk about pigmies and kittens and religion. I'm fed up."

CHAPTER SEVEN

EASTER SUNDAY dawned bright and beautiful. Pauline gazed through the window at the golden sunshine on the flowers and trees. Even the birds seemed to know that it was a special day, and as though she wished to play her part in the Easter story, a mother hen passed the house followed by her six fluffy yellow chicks.

"They're just like Easter-egg chickens," said Pauline to Stephen, "only much nicer because they're real."

At breakfast everyone found a boiled egg in a beautiful new egg-cup and covered with a tiny cosy, specially knitted by Mrs. Rogers. Even Ann was intrigued, and when she was told that they were her very own and to be taken away with her whenever she left, she had a sudden recollection of the gift she was supposed to be giving, and which she had recently destroyed in order that the children should never receive it. But she tried to brush aside the thought, and was unusually gay and talkative. However, she found herself troubled again by the reading after breakfast, when Mr. Rogers opened his Bible. The words were strangely exciting and created a vivid picture in the child's mind. For the first time she paid attention to the reading:

"In the end of the sabbath as it began to dawn toward the first day of the week, came Mary Magdalene and the other Mary to see the sepulchre. And behold, there was a great earthquake: for the angel of the Lord descended from heaven and came and rolled back the stone from the door, and sat upon it. His countenance was like lightning and his raiment white as snow. And for fear of him the keepers did shake, and became as dead men. And the angel answered and said unto the women, Fear not ye: for I know that ye seek Jesus, which was crucified. He is not here: for He is risen, as He said, Come, see the place where the Lord lay."

Strange words to attract a small girl, yet in this word picture she could see the angel of the Lord, like lightning, and she could feel the force of the earthquake, and she could feel the terror of the keepers. She wondered if this terrible angel might appear to her and accuse her of keeping back that money. She was sure he must know everything, and so began a great fear which grew and grew during that Easter Sunday.

Ann did not enjoy Sunday very much at any time. She liked having no school, but she found

going to church a dull business. This Easter
Sunday church time came round as usual. Stephen
had been particularly annoying, talking and asking
questions instead of eating his breakfast, and then
when all were ready he managed, at the last
minute, to fall into a bucket of water, and so had
to be quickly changed. Pauline and Ann waited
while Mr. Rogers went on ahead to start the
service. It was some ten minutes later that they
arrived, and even before reaching the church they
could hear the singing.

"Isn't it lovely?" said Pauline. "I love Easter
hymns almost as much as Christmas ones."

"I don't," said Stephen, for no other reason
than that he wanted to disagree with someone.
"I like GOOD KING WENCESLAS best, all about
the poor man in the snow."

"That's not a hymn," scoffed Pauline.

"It is then," said Stephen, now on the threshold
of the church. "It's in the book of carols."

Mrs. Rogers managed to silence him, and they
entered amid a volume of harmony and praise—
such a glorious rejoicing. The hymn seemed to be
endless, and the people never tired of singing.
Never before had Ann felt so out of things. She
could see Baba Eliya, singing his head off, and
Rebeka among the girls singing her head off, and
beside her was Pauline doing likewise. As she did
not understand much of the language, her hymn-

book did not help her much, so at the end of the hymn she whispered to Pauline:

"What was that about?"

"In English," explained Pauline, "it is 'Christ the Lord is risen today'."

Ann did not understand much about that, but she knew that the reading after breakfast had been about Christ being risen, and she felt horribly conscious again of the angel whose countenance was like lightning.

Encouraged by Ann's first question, Pauline occasionally translated parts of the message too, and this was all right until she explained, "He is saying now about a verse of the Bible 'Thou God seest me'."

Ann felt hot and uncomfortable. This is what she feared. God knew all about her. That dreadful angel knew all about her, and would surely come and accuse her. How she wished she had not destroyed those cheques. Even now, she could have given them to the children. She was glad when they left the church and all walked back to the house together, including Miss Brown, who was coming for lunch. In the house Miss Brown produced three little parcels, one for each child. Ann slowly opened hers and found inside a beautiful New Testament with gilt edges and lettering. Pauline was shouting "Thank You" with great joy, but Ann did not know what to say, so she said solemnly, "Thank you very much," and walked into her bedroom, where she put the beautiful little book on her bedside table. It scared her to look at it. In there she could read all about the angel of the Lord if she wished, but she did not wish, and so she left it unopened. She forgot the other things she had read out of the New Testament—beautiful stories of Jesus and His love—she just remembered that God saw her and knew her sin, and she wanted to run away from the house and all the people in it, and find her daddy, who would help her to forget these dreadful things.

It was evening when they were all sitting quietly talking—that is all except Stephen. Suddenly they heard a shriek, and in a moment Mrs. Rogers turned pale. What had Stephen done now? But the next minute, just as she was about to go out to him, in he rushed with his hands full of something. Flushed and excited, he charged into the midst of the company.

"They've come," he said triumphantly, and deposited four tiny, new-born kittens on the table, while poor Tibby, distracted, jumped up and began licking them desperately.

"Oh, do take them back," cried Mrs. Rogers, but Pauline swooped down on them and gathered them up, allowing Tibby to get hold of one and carry it back to bed.

66

"Stephen will kill them all before he's finished," she cried, and so the tiny things were safely put back for the night.

Stephen went to bed radiantly happy. "They're Easter kittens," he said drowsily, as his mother tucked him in.

CHAPTER EIGHT

IT was half-past four in the afternoon, a hot afternoon, heavy with the heaviness of an approaching storm, though as yet there was no sign of rain. Easter was over. The pigmies had returned the day before, and Pauline, missing her small charges, had gone to see Miss Brown.

Rebeka left home with her young brother, both children carrying armfuls of fresh corn, whose silken tassels fluttered gracefully in the faint breeze which occasionally blew across the compound. In the distance they could hear the faint rumbling of thunder. When they reached the missionaries' house they found Stephen sitting on the edge of the veranda watching Tibby with her kittens, whose box he had brought out of the house.

"Where's your mother?" asked Rebeka.

"At the dispensary," said Stephen, without looking up.

"Your father, then?"

"Building," came the brief reply.

"And your sister?"

"Gone to see Miss Brown."

It was only then that Stephen looked up and caught sight of the corn.

"Is that for us?" he asked, smiling with pleasure, and on learning that it was, he said, "Good-oh," and then as an afterthought added, "Thank you."

Having thus accomplished her task, Rebeka sat down too on the veranda, swinging her slim brown legs. "Who's having those kittens?" she asked.

"I don't really know yet," said Stephen thoughtfully. "They're rather special."

"Why?" asked Rebeka, looking for some special mark upon them.

"They're Easter kittens," explained Stephen, "and may cost a lot of money."

"Oh," said Rebeka. "We need a cat. The rats eat our food and our clothes too."

Stephen was very conscious of the pile of corn near by and felt a little obliged to say that maybe he would give them a kitten when it was old enough.

Thus encouraged and cheered, Rebeka began to sing, a native melody which her brother and Stephen both joined in. They did not know that from her bedroom Ann was listening to them, and that overhearing their friendly chatter and now listening to the harmony and rhythm of this simple tune, she felt shut out and lonely. She would not have acknowledged that she was jealous of Rebeka as she also was of the pigmies. It was really this which made her almost hate them, and because people with hatred in their hearts cannot be happy, Ann had no joy and could not bear to see them joyful. She had always been little girl number ONE, and she did not like being anything else. So because she could not bear to hear the children singing happily together, she shouted through the window:

"I wish you would go and sing your native songs somewhere else."

Then she sat down, and waited for the result.

The children were so amazed at hearing a voice coming from nowhere, they stopped singing immediately, but as Stephen understood what she had said, he quickly started them singing again, but louder this time. Rebeka grinned, for she guessed what Ann had said, and Stephen caught her eye and grinned back. Furiously, Ann picked up the nearest object to hand, which proved to be a rather large dictionary, and going to the window she threw it at them—but instead of hitting the children it fell in the box of kittens, terrifying Tibby and temporarily hurting a kitten so that it lay still and apparently lifeless. Had it not been for the kitten, things may have even then passed off without further trouble, but on seeing one of Tibby's Easter kittens lying so helpless, Stephen stood up and shouted:

"You horrible, mean thing, you cruel, horrid thing, killing a tiny kitten."

Ann was a little scared when she heard this, but she refused to acknowledge it. "Pooh," she said. "Who wants your stupid kittens, anyway?"

Trembling and angry, Stephen tried to say all the things he had ever thought about Ann. "I hate you," he cried. "You're nothing but an old spoil sport, and now you can't leave the kittens alone just because they belong to someone else. If you don't like them, I do—I love them—so do we all, which is more than we can say about you. We'll all be glad when you go back again."

He was hot and red-faced, and his words did not come out quite so smoothly as that, for he stuttered in his rage. But this did not prevent his hot words from doing their work. In his rage he had included both his father and mother, Pauline and Rebeka in this desire to see Ann go. He had no idea what might be the consequences of such rash words, for words are dangerous things—we can never un-say them. Seeing the kitten revive, Stephen calmed down, and in the joy of relief he quite forgot Ann. But Ann did not forget. Tears of hurt pride and anger welled up in her eyes. She had only one desire—to get away from the house. Nobody wanted her. That was what Stephen had said—and knowing how bad she had often been, Ann did not doubt that this was true. If no one wanted her she would run away. Her father was somewhere beyond the forest—maybe if she

71

hurried she could get through the forest and find him. Poor Ann did not realise that the great forest of Africa stretched for miles, and her father was a long, long way off. For a few minutes she was afraid at the thought of the forest, especially that bridge of logs which had been so hard to cross, but she was desperate to get to her father and to run away from the missionaries' house. Maybe once she was away she would be able to forget the money she had refused to give to the children, and the day she had tripped up Stephen when he was walking over the bridge and the number of times she had been proud and selfish— most of all, maybe she would be able to forget that awful text—"Thou God seest me". So because of her fear of being found out and the idea that no one wanted her, she forgot her fear of the forest and slipped out of the house unnoticed. Soon she was away from the compound, having been careful to avoid being seen by natives, who would be sure to follow her.

How cool it seemed in the forest, but before long she realised that it was also getting dark. The sun was going down, and she began to wonder if she would ever find her way. Also, she heard the rumble of thunder, and several flashes of lightning scared her. All at once she did not care very much about running away, and turning round, started to walk back. As she turned, she tripped over a small log and fell. A sharp pain in her ankle made her cry out—and when she tried to stand up she fell down again because of the pain. She tried hopping along, but it was impossible in the forest, so many things got in the way. She fell down, exhausted, not bearing to move her leg an inch, and she was glad to lean back against a tree. Around her she heard the forest noises. How clear and close they seemed. She heard the piercing noises of the insects, and near by the croak of a bull frog. How dark it had become—and how cold. Ann shuddered, partly through cold, partly through fear. She wondered if she would ever be found. Probably they would never think to look for her in the forest, and she was filled with dread. A cold wind was driving through the forest now, a wind which is the harbinger of a storm. But worst of all was the terrifying scream of the small animal which climbs the palm-trees at night. As it climbed higher and higher, so its scream became louder and louder. It was quite dark now, and Ann felt that something, or someone, was creeping near her. She felt that eyes were watching her, yet she could not have said why. Hardly daring to breathe, in case she missed some slight noise, she sat tense and terrified. For the first time, she found herself praying to God. She hardly knew how, but she knew that if God could see her, maybe He would help her. She was afraid He was very angry with her because of the bad things she had done and said, so she said:

"Please, God, I know I have been very bad, and you know all about it. Please forgive me and help me now to get out of the forest."

She did not know anything else to say, though slowly memories of things which she had heard at the missionaries' house came back to her. There was the story of the Good Shepherd who searched for the lost sheep. She knew the Shepherd was Jesus, and she now understood that she was the lost sheep. Oh, if only He would find her and save her, she would be so different in future. It would be dreadful never to be forgiven for stealing someone else's money—and Ann knew that that is what she had done, even though she had not kept those cheques for herself. A great crash of thunder startled her, and she sank to the ground, weeping and fearful.

CHAPTER NINE

IT was almost supper-time when everybody missed Ann. Mrs. Rogers went around the house looking for her, and Pauline walked about shouting her name at the top of her voice.

"Where can she be?" cried Mrs. Rogers.

When they saw darkness creeping on, they began to be alarmed and sent the 'boys' to look all over the compound for her. They called Baba Eliya, but he had not seen her, neither had anyone else. As they were discussing what could be done to find her, a man came running up to them. In the native dialect he explained something to Baba Eliya. He was obviously greatly disturbed, and they all saw the look of concern with which Baba Eliya received his message. The man had run from a nearby village, and was breathless and exhausted.

"He has brought news that there is a leopard roaming around," explained Baba Eliya. "It has entered a village not far away and was chased off into the forest, but they feel it is making for this direction. We are to warn people to stay indoors during the dark."

No one said anything for a few seconds. Everybody's thoughts were upon the same things—the fact that Ann was not with them, and a leopard was near at hand. At that moment another messenger arrived. A bright flash of lightning showed him up clearly as he reached them, and everyone gasped with surprise.

"It's the pigmy," cried Pauline.

"It's Tutu," cried Stephen.

Tutu also told Baba Eliya his news and at this they saw his face more concerned than ever.

"He says the white child is in the forest," explained Baba Eliya, "and if we will go he will lead us to her. He says she cannot walk."

Ann was in the forest! The leopard had been chased into the forest, and was believed to be coming that way! What fear gripped everyone at these two pieces of news, and how many prayers went up silently as they set about arranging to fetch Ann. If she could not walk they must arrange something on which to carry her. They looked at the dark sky, and as the thunder became louder, they wondered if they could reach her before the storm broke.

"Whatever would send her into the forest," said Mrs. Rogers, as she prepared Ann's bed by putting in hot bottles.

She knew the little girl would be suffering from fear and cold when she returned. Pauline wanted to do something too, for she was terribly upset at the thought of Ann being in such danger, and wondered how she would feel if she were stranded in the dark forest in a storm. Going to her room, she knelt down and simply asked the Lord Jesus to take care of Ann and bring her back safely. As she arose, she saw Stephen. He was standing watching her, and his eyes were large with fear. His voice was husky as he spoke.

"Will it kill her?" he asked.

Pauline knew what he meant. "Oh, Stephen, don't be horrid," she cried.

"I'm not being horrid," said the little boy. "I want to know."

Pauline tried to sound convincing. "I have just asked Jesus to take care of her," she said, "and I believe He will."

She saw that Stephen was not so easily impressed. Suddenly he burst out crying. Pauline knew it was not from any affection for Ann—it was because of fear, and she put her arm round him and drew him towards her.

"What is the matter, Stephen?" she asked.

For a long while he could not speak, then between sobs his voice came to her muffled and shaky. "I'm scared 'cos I told her to go away. I said none of us wanted her."

Having made his confession, Stephen felt a load had lifted, but he was too scared to face Pauline.

Pauline was horrified. "Why ever did you say that?" she asked.

" 'Cos she tried to kill one of the kittens," said the little boy. "I didn't mean her to go and run into the forest. But it's true, I did want her to go."

Pauline felt sorry for him, although his words had caused such trouble.

Stephen leaned against her and continued, "You said to me one day that if I didn't love everybody I'd never go to Heaven."

"Did I say that?" asked the astonished Pauline.

"Yes, you said a Christian loves everybody."

Pauline could see now why Stephen was so worried. He had a double worry—that of not loving Ann and that of having caused her to run away because of his words, words which had not been true. He knew that no one else felt quite as he did, although Pauline had often had difficulty in trying to be a sister to Ann, which is what Mrs. Rogers said she should be.

"I can't say I ALWAYS love her," said Pauline, wishing to be quite honest in view of Stephen's open confession. "But when I asked the Lord Jesus to forgive me and to help me to love her, He did."

Stephen sighed deeply. "Do you think——? Oh, how awful if that leopard kills her," he cried. "They'll say it's my fault, and God won't forgive me."

"Don't be silly," said his sister. "The best

78

thing to do is to ask Him now, and we will tell Him we are trusting Him to look after Ann."

Stephen seemed relieved at this suggestion, and obediently did as Pauline said, but it was a very restless little boy who went to bed that evening, and he tossed about sleeplessly.

Meanwhile the men had gone with Mr. Rogers and had reached the spot where Ann lay. By the light of their lamps they gently lifted her on to the improvised stretcher, but even so, Ann cried out with pain and fear. She was so relieved to see them after the dreadful tension of lying there in the dark, she began to cry pitifully. As they were about to begin the journey home, Mr. Rogers saw a small figure appear from behind a tree! Then he saw another one and yet another. They seemed to appear from nowhere. What were they doing at this hour, out in the forest? Shyly they stood at a distance, holding their bows and arrows.

"The pigmies," said Mr. Rogers to Baba Eliya. "What are they doing?"

Baba Eliya smiled. "They've been guarding the child," he explained. "Tutu found her in the dark—she couldn't see him, but he saw her. He called these others and they have been standing guard. No harm could have come to her."

Mr. Rogers was silent for a long time. "Please will you tell them how very thankful we are to them!" he said at last. "Especially to the one who came with the message. They have probably saved this child's life."

The pigmies gazed solemnly at Baba Eliya as he translated this into their own dialect. He also informed them that the leopard might be near, and it would be best to go home quickly, but they said they hoped to see it, as they intended killing it, and one man produced his long spear to show that they meant business.

On the way home, they felt the first drops of rain, and the men hurried as much as possible. By the time Ann was safely in the house, the rain had come heavily and lightning was frequent. There was a great clap of thunder overhead, and the rain poured down in earnest. Ann was attended to and put to bed. How wonderful it was to be in the warm bed and to drink steaming hot cocoa, with Mrs. Rogers and Pauline lovingly taking care of her. It was worth having sprained her ankle to receive such attention.

Before they left her, Ann called Mrs. Rogers to stay behind a while. "I want to say something," she said shyly, so Mrs. Rogers waited patiently.

Then Ann explained everything—how frightened she had been Easter Sunday because she knew God knew all about her—how she had kept back the cheques which her father had sent—how she had tripped up Stephen going over the bridge and how she had always hated the people whom

Pauline had liked. Yes, that was it. She longed desperately for Pauline's friendship, yet had given so little herself. She knew she had been bad to Stephen and Rebeka and had said things about the pigmies because Pauline seemed more interested in them than in her. As she mentioned the pigmies, she coloured and turned her face away. Her large blue eyes filled with tears.

"I feel so awful," she sobbed. "They saved my life tonight—Mr. Rogers said so. Oh, I wish I could be a Christian and be happy like Pauline."

This cry came from her heart, and found a response in Mrs. Rogers' heart. Taking the little girl's hand in her own, she said:

"But you can be a Christian, dear. You have told me what is in your heart. Why not tell the Lord Jesus and ask Him to give you a new, clean heart? Pauline had to do that, so have we all. We are none of us Christians without having the bad things cleansed away by Jesus."

Quite simply, and desperately believing in what Mrs. Rogers had said, Ann closed her eyes and prayed. It was a very simple little prayer, but God heard her, and she knew the Good Shepherd had found her. Mrs. Rogers' eyes filled with tears —tears of joy that this little lamb had come into the fold. She had often wondered if they would ever reach Ann's heart, but the miracle had happened, and she could see by Ann's eyes as she turned them upon herself, that she was full of joy. Kissing the child, she quietly left the room, and found Pauline.

"Go in to say 'Good night' to Ann," she said.

Pauline went quietly to the door and knocked.

"Come in," said Ann—a little nervously—for she knew it was Pauline and she hardly knew what to say.

"Hello," said Pauline brightly. "Are you all right now?"

Ann began to laugh softly. "Yes, I'm all right—now," she said. Then shyly she said, "I've just asked the Lord Jesus to give me a new heart."

Haltingly, she told Pauline what she had told her mother.

"Stephen can't get to sleep for worrying," said Pauline. "He says he sent you away, and he feels so bad about it."

Ann smiled. "I don't feel bad about anything now," she said. "Tell Stephen to stop worrying. Anyway, it was my own fault. I've always been horrid to him. You'd better ask HIM if he will forgive ME."

Pauline found Stephen hot and restless. "Don't worry about Ann," she said. "She's all right, and she says I'm to ask you to forgive her for all the bad things she's said to you. She says it's her own fault she ran away."

Stephen felt better after that. He had so feared

what Ann would say about him and what Ann's father would say—and do—if she told him what had happened. As usual, at night, things had seemed to get worse and worse as he thought about them. Turning over with a big sigh, he went to sleep.

CHAPTER TEN

TWO weeks later Ann's father came to fetch her. How differently Ann awaited his arrival, from the day when she had longed for her father to take her away. She felt now a queer little pain inside—a sadness which hovered over her each time she thought of leaving. For she knew she would be leaving for good, leaving Mrs. Rogers, who was now a mother to her, and Pauline, who was now a sister. Even Stephen would be missed, for Ann was a new child, and in place of the old hatred was love, and in place of the desire to be always first, she found herself willing to be last. She had moments when the old Ann tried to appear again, but Mrs. Rogers always helped her over these difficult times and taught her to pray about everything.

Stephen had tried to mend his ways too, and had gone so far as to offer Ann one of Tibby's Easter kittens. Ann sat with the tiny creature on her lap now, and tears came to her eyes. She couldn't take it with her. It would stay behind like everyone else, while she went away to England and to school.

"Will you write to me?" she asked Pauline.

"Of course," said Pauline. "And you must write and tell me what you do in England."

"When will you be going to England?" asked Ann.

"Daddy says we'll be going some time this year, but he's not sure when," replied Pauline. "We'll be able to see each other again then."

Ann cheered up a little, and presently her father's car appeared. She felt that she was leaving home, and clung to Mrs. Rogers as though she could never leave her. But eventually off they went. Ann hanging out of the car and waving until they were out of sight. She looked at the distant forest and remembered her adventure, an adventure which had ended in the joy of finding the Saviour. She thought of the pigmies who had cared for her, although she had never once shown them kindness—the little people of the forest who needed people to care for them and to teach them.

"Well, Ann," said her father brightly. "Make the most of Africa during the next day or two, for you'll be leaving it behind for good."

"I wonder," thought Ann, and she felt a big lump in her throat, for they had now left behind the bit of Africa she knew, and were speeding along, rushing away from all that had become familiar to her, rushing into a new life which would be filled with new people whom she did not know.

Pauline wandered slowly towards Miss Brown's house. It was evening, and the world seemed bathed in golden sunlight as the sun went down. The beautiful blue kingfisher darted past her, giving his sharp call as he did so often early in the morning. The small birds in the palms were having their last twitter before retiring for the night when she saw Baba Eliya and Rebeka hurrying towards her. Baba Eliya was carrying something so peculiar—but as they drew near Pauline saw that it was the skin of a leopard, complete with tail. She gazed at it in astonishment.

"What are you doing with that?" she asked, as they reached her.

"It is for you," explained Baba Eliya, smiling. "It is a gift—the coat of the leopard which was around here the other week."

"For me," cried Pauline, flushing with pleasure, as she looked at the shining coat with its beautiful markings. "From whom?"

"From your friends the pigmies," said Baba Eliya and Rebeka together.

At that moment Pauline heard something that made her turn round quickly—it was the continual ringing of a bicycle bell, and sure enough there was Stephen careering along in a very wobbly fashion as he could not reach the saddle. He was flushed and looked very scared as he reached Pauline, but as he did not know how to stop he collapsed before her together with the bicycle. Pauline picked him up and brushed him. "What are you doing?" she exclaimed.

Stephen was too excited and too shaken with his fall to speak clearly, but he managed to say jerkily, "Isn't—it—wonderful—— We found it after they'd gone—Ann's bicycle with a message—for me—she says I'm to have it."

He paused to get more breath and brush back unruly hair.

"How lovely!" cried Pauline. "She wants to show that she really is different now since she became a Christian. I do wish she could have stayed here."

"Oh, I don't know," said Stephen honestly. "She might not have given me her bicycle."

Pauline gasped and opened her mouth to rebuke her young brother, but he seemed so unaware of what he had said that she only said in desperation, "Really, Stephen!" She watched him start off again on the bicycle, wobbling dangerously. "Really!" she exclaimed again with a little smile.